花 木 兰 的 故 事
——中国古代女英雄

The Legend of Mu Lan
A Heroine of Ancient China

姜 巍　姜 成 安　编绘

written and illustrated by
Jiang, Wei and **Jiang, Cheng An**

胜利出版社
Victory Press

Victory Press
543 Lighthouse Avenue
Monterey, CA 93940
(408) 883-1725
(408) 883-8710 fax

ISBN: 1-878217-14-3

Printed in Hong Kong by South China Printing, Ltd.

Library of Congress Cataloging-in-Publication Data

Chiang, Wei, 1969 -
    [Hua Mu-lan ti ku shih: Chong-kuo ku tai nu ying hsiung / pien hsieh, hui hua Chiang Wei, Chiang Ch'eng-an] = The legend of Mu Lan : a heroine of ancient China / written and illustrated by Jiang, Wei and Jiang, Cheng An
          p.   cm.
    Chinese and English.
    Based on: Mu-lan Shih.
    Title and author statement in Chinese characters.
    Summary: A bilingual folktale, based on a poem from the Song Dynasty, in which a young girl disguises herself as a man and leads the army of China to victory against the enemy.

    ISBN 1-878217-14-3 : $7.95
    1. Hua, Mu-lan (Legendary character) - -Legends. [1. Folklore- -China. 2. Chinese language materials --Bilingual.] I. Chiang, Cheng An   II. Mu-lan shih.   III. Title.   IV. Title: Legend of Mu Lan.
GR335.4.H83C47 1992   91-24610
398.21' 0951--dc20   CIP
                                                                                            AC

很久以前，在古代中国的农村里，有一个女孩子名叫花木兰。她聪颖好学
。

Long ago in a farming village in ancient China, there lived a girl named Mu Lan. She was smart and brave.

花木兰自幼跟着父亲学武健身，练就一身好武艺，刀枪棍棒，样样皆通，骑马射箭，百发百中。

Since she was young, her father taught her to fight with swords, spears and poles. She also learned to ride horseback and shoot with a bow and arrow. She was good in all different types of martial arts.

这日，花木兰的父亲接到皇帝派人送来的军书，讲边境敌人来犯，形势非常紧张，要父亲再赴战场。

One day a messenger appeared at the door. He had an order from the emperor for Mu Lan's father, General Hua. Enemies from the north were invading China and the situation was serious. Mu Lan's father was ordered to return to the front lines to fight.

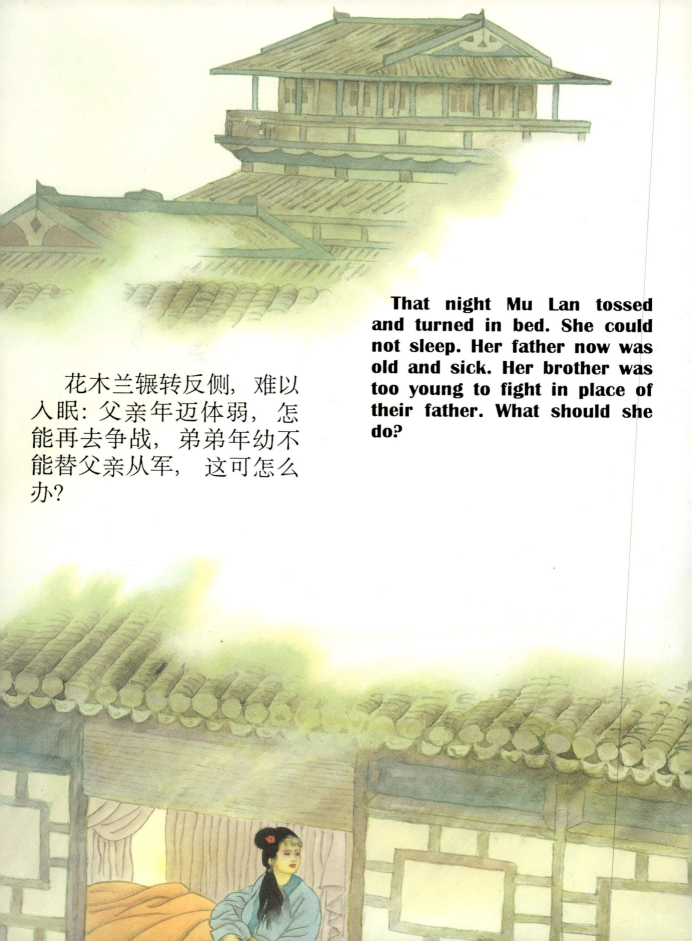

花木兰辗转反侧，难以入眠：父亲年迈体弱，怎能再去争战，弟弟年幼不能替父亲从军，这可怎么办？

That night Mu Lan tossed and turned in bed. She could not sleep. Her father now was old and sick. Her brother was too young to fight in place of their father. What should she do?

Mu Lan got up from her bed and went to the courtyard. She could hear her parents sigh in their room.

花木兰再也躺不住了，她起床来到院子里，侧耳听见父母正叹息不止。

花木兰越发不安了，她进屋说：“二老不用发愁，木兰愿替父应征。”父亲摇头说：“朝廷有明文规定，不要女子！行不通，行不通！”

Mu Lan entered their room and said, "Father, Mother, don't worry. I can fight for father." General Hua shook his head as he replied, "The law says females are not allowed to join the army. It is impossible."

次日清晨，一个英姿飒爽的青年军人站在父母面前："二老请看，女儿能上前线吗？" 弟弟木礼惊叫道："原来是姐姐女扮男装啊！"

The next morning a sharply dressed young soldier stood before General and Mrs. Hua, and asked, "Father, Mother, now can I join the battle ranks?" "Oh! It's you Mu Lan, dressed as a soldier!" Mu Li, Mu Lan's younger brother cried out in surprise.

父母高兴地流下了眼泪，再也没有别的办法了只好点头同意。父亲说：“木兰儿，你替父从军，实乃可喜。不过沙场之上戎马倥偬，箭飞来飞去，非同儿戏，你可要多加小心。”木兰说：“请爹爹放心。”

Tears rolled down the faces of Mu Lan's parents. They nodded and agreed to let Mu Lan fight against the northern invaders. "Mu Lan, I am proud that you are willing to take my place in battle," General Hua said. Then he cautioned, "But on the front lines battle horses gallop wildly and arrows fly ceaselessly. It is not child's play. You must be careful." "Father don't worry," Mu Lan replied.

花木兰嘱咐弟弟听话，
要多帮父母干活，然后跨
上骏马，雄赳赳地加入了
应征的行列。

**Mu Lan told her brother to
take care of their parents while
she was gone. Then she
mounted a battle horse and
bravely entered the ranks of
soldiers.**

"这不是花老将军的儿子花木礼吗?" 花木兰听见同伴问自己, 就应声答道: "在下正是花木礼。" 花木兰顶弟弟名替父从军。

"Are you General Hua's son, Mu Li?" asked a companion. "Yes, I am," answered Mu Lan without hesitation. Thus, Mu Lan joined the military using her brother's name.

一路上，花木兰和伙伴们晓行夜宿，风尘仆仆地来到边关。

Mu Lan and her companions traveled for days and days over windy and dusty plains. They finally reached the northern frontier.

花木兰武艺高强，在刀光剑影中，横枪跃马，左右开弓，令敌人丧胆，使同伴们折服。

Mu Lan was skilled in martial arts. Whether wielding a sword in hand -to-hand combat, gallop-ing on horseback with a spear or shooting an arrow, she always could frighten the enemy. Her companions all admired her ability.

因她有胆有识，惯战，屡立战功，又懂演阵兵法，很快就提升为扫北上将军。

Because of her courage, intelligence and ability, she was successful in many battles. Since she was also well versed in military strategy, soon she was promoted to the rank of commanding general.

One day Mu Lan led troops to Mount Mo Tein (present day Cheng De city in He Bei Province in China). The enemy had already occupied the steep cliff and were camping on top. It seemed almost impossible to attack the enemy from the base of the mountain.

　　这日，花木兰率兵马扫北来到中国现在的承德东北的摩天岭，只见悬崖峭壁，敌兵屯居山上，从下面休想攻得上去。

花木兰回到大帐，想起自己从军已十年了，十分怀念爹娘和小弟，怀念乡亲们，恨不得一脚蹋平摩天岭，早日班师回朝。

Mu Lan returned to her tent and thought. She had been fighting for over ten years. She missed her parents, younger brother and other relatives. She wished she could flatten Mount Mo Tien in one step and lead her troops home.

暮霭苍茫，天色昏暗，
花木兰趁黑夜率领将士观
察地形。

**At dusk, while the sky was
dark, Mu Lan led officers out
to survey the battle situation.**

花木兰立马高处眺望，只见山顶上敌营内灯火熠熠，人影闪动，阵阵胡笳声随风传过。

Sitting on her horse, Mu Lan could see the blinking lights from the enemy's camp on the peak. Shadows moved within the tents and the faint sound of the enemy's military bugle floated down with the wind.

木兰正在凝思，突然一声"咩－－"的羊叫声，把她吓了一跳。

Mu Lan was quietly thinking when she was startled by a long, ''Bbaaahh.''

只见一群羊正在陡峭的
山上蹦来跳去，花木兰想：
"羊有那样好的爬山本领，
我何不用羊灯计破摩天领
呢!"

She looked up and saw a
herd of goats playing on the
slope of the mountain. Mu Lan
thought, "Goats can climb up
mountains. Why don't I use
them to attack the enemies on
Mount Mo Ten?"

第二天，花木兰升帐调
兵遣将，让他们四处买羊
。

The next day, Mu Lan gathered the officers and men in her tent. She ordered some of them to buy as many goats as they could find.

花木兰又命人找来扎纸
匠人，日夜赶糊大批灯笼
。

She ordered others to hire craftsmen to work day and night making paper lanterns.

她又在附近访问当地山
民，找出了一条登山的小
路。

By asking the local people, she was able to find a small path leading up to the top of the mountain.

在一个漆黑的夜里，花木兰让将士们在每只羊角上挂上灯笼，把羊群赶上摩天岭。

One pitch dark night, Mu Lan ordered the officers to hang a lantern on each goat's horn, then to drive the goats up the mountain.

羊群漫山遍野往山上跑，山上的敌兵一见，以为是花木兰攻山的人马，便齐放滚木擂石。

The goats bound up the cliff from all different directions. When the enemy saw the moving light, they thought General Hua's troops were attacking. They quickly got logs and large boulders and pushed them down the mountain.

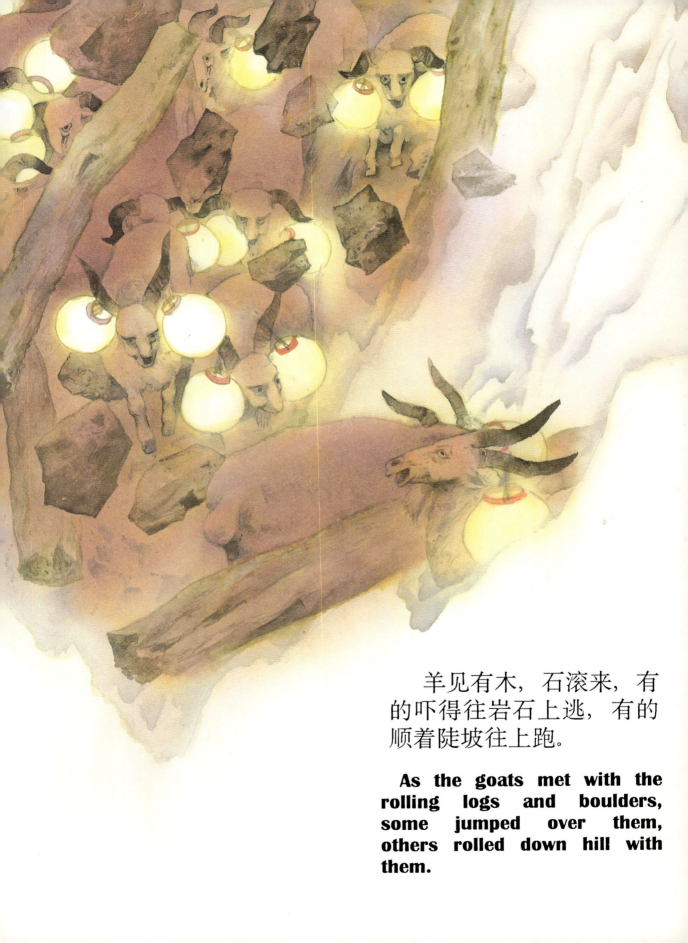

羊见有木，石滚来，有
的吓得往岩石上逃，有的
顺着陡坡往上跑。

**As the goats met with the
rolling logs and boulders,
some jumped over them,
others rolled down hill with
them.**

这下可把敌将吓坏啦：人怎么登险石而上？难道是天兵？敌兵将不明真相，一时乱了阵脚。

This really frightened the officers of the enemy camp. They thought, "How could people jump over rolling boulders? They must be soldiers from heaven."

At this time, Mu Lan led her troops up the little mountain path and attacked the enemy. Many of them were killed. Some surrendered. Some escaped to their own kingdom. But no one dared to return to invade the Chinese border again.

花木兰率领众将官乘机从小路攻上去，把敌兵杀得逃的逃，降的降，一气跑回本国，再也不敢来侵犯边境了。

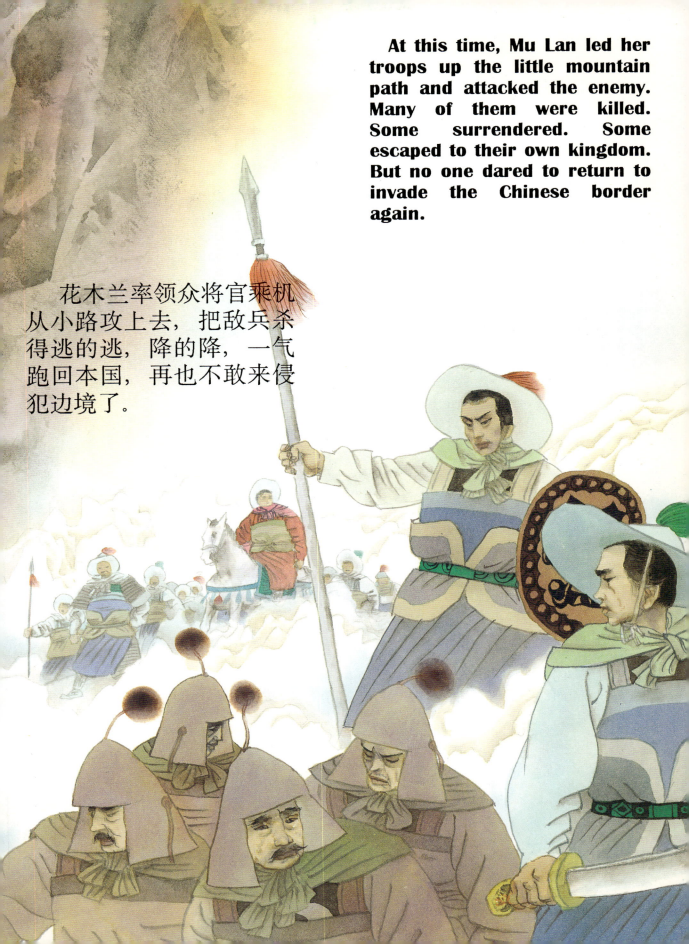

花木兰大获全胜，班师回朝。

Mu Lan was completely victorious. She lead her triumphant troops back to report to the emperor.

　　皇帝要给花木兰将军封
官进爵，但她一一谢绝。

The emperor offered Mu Lan a higher position in the government, but she politely declined. She requested to be sent home.

花木兰解甲归里，还了女儿身。当同伴们知道这位英俊赫赫有名的花将军，原来是一位亭亭玉立的女子时，无不惊讶万分。花木兰替父从军和荣立战功的事迹就这样广泛流传开来了。

Mu Lan returned to her farming village and handed over her military uniform to the soldiers accompanying her. When they saw she was really a female, their surprise was boundless. From this time on, the story of Mu Lan spread throughout China.